Differently
the
Same

JESSICA GAYLE SIBANDA

Illustrations inspired by Cindy Gayle Bell

Trilogy Christian Publishers
A Wholly Owned Subsidary of Trinity Broadcasting Network
2442 Michelle Drive
Tustin, CA 92780

For information, address Trilogy Christian Publishing
Rights Department, 2442 Michelle Drive, Tustin, Ca 92780.
Trilogy Christian Publishing/ TBN and colophon are trademarks of Trinity Broadcasting Network.

For information about special discounts for bulk purchases, please contact Trilogy Christian Publishing.

Manufactured in the United States of America

Trilogy Disclaimer: The views and content expressed in this book are those of the author and may not necessarily reflect the views and doctrine of Trilogy Christian Publishing or the Trinity Broadcasting Network.

10 9 8 7 6 5 4 3 2 1

Library of Congress Cataloging-in-Publication Data is available.

ISBN 978-1-64773-480-0 (Print Book)
ISBN 978-1-64773-481-7 (ebook)

Dedication

To my husband, James. Thanks for believing in me, supporting my dreams, and loving me.

Thinking about the first day of school was exciting and a little bit scary for Sophia. Sophia's parents told her great things about starting school. Sophia would get to learn new things and make new friends. But, since Sophia had never been to school, she was nervous.

Sophia wondered what it would be like to have friends. She had never been around other chinchillas her age, and she was afraid they would not like her.

The first day of school came, and Sophia woke up extra early. She ate breakfast, brushed her teeth, and put on a dress she and her mother had bought just for this special day. It was purple—her favorite color—with turquoise polka dots. Sophia was ready to go to school.

When Sophia got to the school, she was surprised to see that many of the other chinchillas looked very different than she did. Sophia was a gray chinchilla, and so was everyone in her family. Sophia had never seen a chinchilla that was not gray.

As Sophia looked around at chinchillas with brown, black, and white fur, she became even more scared and turned and asked her mom if they could go home.

Sophia's mom asked her, "What's the matter, Honey?"

Sophia whispered, "Mommy, I do not look like some of these other chinchillas. I don't think I belong here."

Sophia's mother giggled and knelt down to Sophia. "Sophia, chinchillas come in all shapes, sizes, and colors. We may all look different on the outside, but inside, we are all the same. You'll have a great day at school. Just wait and see."

With tears in her eyes, Sophia gave her mom a hug and sat at the desk that had her name written on it. Sophia was nervously watching her mom leave when she was startled by a hand on her shoulder.

Sophia turned to see a black chinchilla wearing a dress just like hers. "I like your dress," laughed the chinchilla. "My name is Sadie. What's your name?"

"My... my... my..." Sophia was so nervous about her first day that she could hardly speak.

"Is your name Sophia?" Sadie asked.

"Yes. How did you know that?"

"I read the name on your desk," replied Sadie.

"Wow! You know how to read?" questioned Sophia.

"Well, I only know a little bit, but my big sister's name is Sophia, so I recognized the letters," explained Sadie.

Just then, the bell rang, and Mrs. Lopez walked to the front of the room. "Welcome to your first day of school," she said. "I am so excited to be your teacher, and I just know we are going to have a great year!"

Little did Sophia know, but she would in fact have a great year! Later that day, Sophia also got to meet many other chinchillas who would soon become her friends.

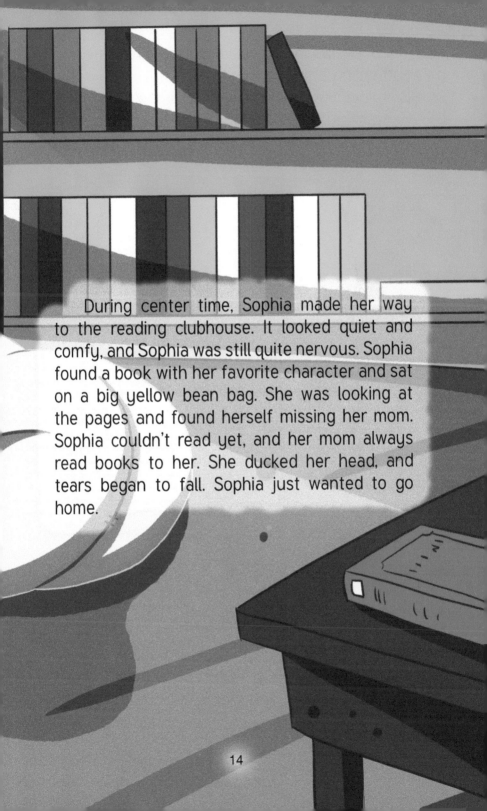

During center time, Sophia made her way to the reading clubhouse. It looked quiet and comfy, and Sophia was still quite nervous. Sophia found a book with her favorite character and sat on a big yellow bean bag. She was looking at the pages and found herself missing her mom. Sophia couldn't read yet, and her mom always read books to her. She ducked her head, and tears began to fall. Sophia just wanted to go home.

Soon, Sophia heard a boy laughing nearby and telling another chinchilla, "Look at her! She is crying!" He was gray, and his name was Chase. He was one of the largest chinchillas in the class. Sophia looked up just as more boys gathered around to laugh at her for crying.

Just when Sophia was set to run away, a brown chinchilla stepped up and stood between Sophia and the group of boys. Fen was a bit smaller than the other boys, but he didn't seem to mind. Fen stood up in the boys' faces and asked them, "Hey guys! Is there something wrong here?"

A couple of the boys turned and walked away, but Chase just kept laughing. He turned to Fen and said, "Oh, are you a crybaby, too?"

Fen said, "I don't see any crybabies around here, but actually, I did cry this morning when my mom left." Chase began laughing even louder. This noise made Mrs. Lopez come over to see what was going on.

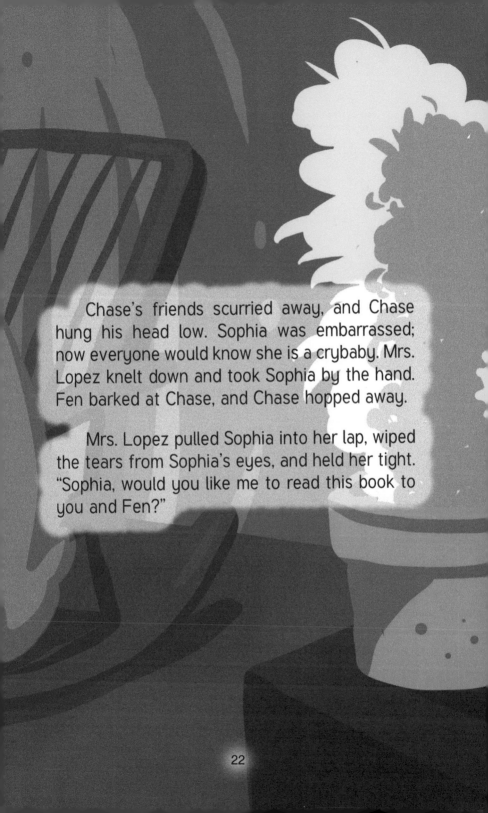

Chase's friends scurried away, and Chase hung his head low. Sophia was embarrassed; now everyone would know she is a crybaby. Mrs. Lopez knelt down and took Sophia by the hand. Fen barked at Chase, and Chase hopped away.

Mrs. Lopez pulled Sophia into her lap, wiped the tears from Sophia's eyes, and held her tight. "Sophia, would you like me to read this book to you and Fen?"

Sophia looked up at Mrs. Lopez. Sophia couldn't believe that her teacher would come and read to her—just like her mom would. Fen looked at Sophia and then at Mrs. Lopez and said, "Yes! I think she would like that!"

Fen and Sophia giggled as Mrs. Lopez read the funny story to them.

At lunch, Sophia was joined by Fen, Sadie, and another friend, Ava. Ava was a spotted chinchilla who was very kind and seemed to be shy like Sophia.

After lunch, Ava, Fen, Sadie, and Sophia ran around on the playground playing tag and enjoying the slides. While waiting on her friends to come down the slide, Sophia felt someone tap her on the back. She turned around and saw Chase.

Sophia was about to take off, but Chase quickly said, "Hold on! I'm here to apologize." Sophia stopped. "I'm really sorry for making fun of you. To be honest, I was ready to cry myself, but I didn't want anyone to make fun of me. So when I saw you crying, instead of crying, I laughed at you. It was a really dumb thing to do, and I just want to say I'm sorry."

About this time, Fen quickly came over ready to come to Sophia's rescue again. "What are you doing here?" Fen asked.

Chase ducked his head. "I just came to tell Sophia that I'm sorry." Then tears started forming in Chase's eyes.

"Hey, Chase! You're it!" Sophia said. Sophia took off running. Chase and Fen looked at each other confused, and they took off running toward Sophia.

Before she knew it, it was the end of the day. Mrs. Lopez walked the class outside, and Sophia saw her mom. She started to run to her, but first, she turned to say good-bye to her new friends. Sophia no longer thought that she didn't fit in. She knew that her mom was right. They may all look different on the outside, but we are differently the same.

Appendix

What is a Chinchilla?

Chinchillas are rodents, and they are native to the Andes Mountains in South America. They are crepuscular animals, which means they are most active in the mornings when the sun is coming up and in the evenings when the sun is setting. They catnap most of the day and night and occasionally get up to eat or get a drink. They are best known for their super soft fur, which is very thick because they are from the mountains where it is cold. Most chinchillas are gray, but they can come in many colors. They were first brought to the United States about one hundred years ago, and many people have them as pets. They are fun to watch as they bounce around and take dust baths.

About the Author

Jessica is a born and raised Texan. She lived in a few other states while in her twenties, then she settled back in Texas where she now resides in the Dallas area. She is married to her husband, James, and they have a daughter, Ella. Jessica has traveled outside of the United States over twenty times serving missionaries and doing humanitarian work. Jessica has a bachelor's degree in English with a social welfare minor and a master's degree in Elementary Education. She was a third grade teacher from 2013 to 2018 with the exception of the 2015 to 2016 school year when she taught kindergarten. Jessica now enjoys being a stay-at-home mom to Ella while writing and running an online children's boutique called The Treasured Lion.